The Raven

Edgar Allan Poe

Adapted and illustrated by Raul Allen

D1602330

Colorist
Borja Pindado

Copyright © 2014 by Scholastic Inc.
All rights reserved. Published by Scholastic Inc.
Printed in the U.S.A.

ISBN-13: 978-0-545-50168-2
ISBN-10: 0-545-50168-7
(meets NASTA specifications)

SCHOLASTIC, SYSTEM 44, and associated logos are trademarks
and/or registered trademarks of Scholastic Inc.
LEXILE is a registered trademark of MetaMetrics, Inc.

7   8   9   10   113   22   21   20   19   18   17   16

Edgar Allan Poe
(1809–1849)

Edgar Allan Poe was an American author. He was born in Boston, Massachusetts, in 1809. His parents died when he was very young. Poe grew up with a foster family, the Allans.

Poe was already writing poems by age 13. He published his first book of poems at age 18. Poe became known for his short stories. He wrote many horror stories. He also wrote many mystery stories.

"The Raven" is Poe's most famous poem. It was published in 1845. It became an instant hit.

Poe died in 1849. He was just 40 years old. No one is sure what caused his death. It is a mystery, just like many of his stories.

About the Poem

"The Raven" is a narrative poem. It tells a story. The story begins on a spooky night. The narrator is lonely and sad. He misses Lenore. She is the love of his life. We don't know what happened to her. Maybe Lenore left him. Maybe she died. Either way, she is gone from his life.

The narrator wants to stop thinking about Lenore. He is reading a book. He hears a knock on the door. Is it Lenore? Has she come back to him? He opens the door. He thinks he hears a voice! But no one is there.

Next, the narrator hears a noise at his window. He opens it. A bird called a raven comes in. The narrator asks the raven its name. The bird answers! "Nevermore," it says. (That means "never again.")

At first, the narrator thinks this answer is funny. A human must have taught the bird this word.

Then, the raven annoys the narrator. It says "nevermore" again and again. The narrator gets fearful and upset. He is really upset when the raven says he will "nevermore" see Lenore. By the end of the poem, the narrator freaks out!

Words and Phrases to Know

balm in Gilead: a lotion made in Gilead, a region in the Middle East. The lotion calms people who are upset.

censer: a metal pot hung from a chain. People burn spices in the pot. The spices make a sweet smell. It fills the air when the pot swings.

chamber: a private room, like a bedroom or office.

nepenthe: a medicine taken to forget sadness.

Pallas: the Greek goddess of wisdom. In the poem, the raven lands on a statue of Pallas's head.

Plutonian shore: the land of the dead. Pluto is a god in Roman myths. He rules the land of the dead.

Think About It

Think about these questions as you read the poem. Why does the narrator smile when he first sees the raven? Why does he get more and more upset as the poem goes on?

1 beguile *verb*
To charm or trick.

*The bird's funny expression could **beguile** any man and cause him to smile.*

2 countenance *noun*
The look on someone's face.

*His face showed a fearful **countenance**.*

3 discourse *noun*
Written or spoken communication.

*Students had a lively **discourse** about the poem.*

4 distinctly *adverb*
Definitely; clearly.

*I remember **distinctly** that it rained last Saturday.*

5

implore *verb*

To beg.

*I **implore** you to leave me alone!*

6 **radiant** *adjective*

Glowing with joy, love, and beauty.

*The man thought his girlfriend looked **radiant**.*

7 **sorrow** *noun*

Great sadness.

*The man felt **sorrow** when he thought about his lost love.*

ONCE UPON A MIDNIGHT DREARY, WHILE I PONDERED, WEAK AND WEARY, OVER MANY A QUAINT AND CURIOUS VOLUME OF FORGOTTEN LORE...

WHILE I NODDED, NEARLY NAPPING,
   SUDDENLY THERE CAME A TAPPING,
AS OF SOME ONE GENTLY RAPPING,
   RAPPING AT MY CHAMBER DOOR.

'Tis some visitor,

I MUTTERED,

tapping at my chamber door—Only this, and nothing more.

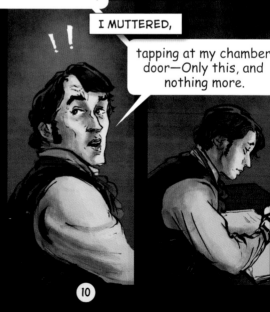

AH, *DISTINCTLY* I REMEMBER IT WAS IN THE BLEAK DECEMBER, AND EACH SEPARATE DYING EMBER WROUGHT ITS GHOST UPON THE FLOOR.

EAGERLY I WISHED THE MORROW;—VAINLY I HAD SOUGHT TO BORROW FROM MY BOOKS SURCEASE OF *SORROW*—SORROW FOR THE LOST LENORE—

FOR THE RARE AND *RADIANT* MAIDEN WHOM THE ANGELS NAME LENORE—NAMELESS HERE FOR EVERMORE.

AND THE SILKEN SAD UNCERTAIN RUSTLING OF EACH PURPLE CURTAIN
THRILLED ME—FILLED ME WITH FANTASTIC TERRORS NEVER FELT BEFORE;

SO THAT NOW, TO STILL THE BEATING OF MY HEART, I STOOD REPEATING,

'Tis some visitor entreating entrance at my chamber door
Some late visitor entreating entrance at my chamber door;—
This it is, and nothing more.

PRESENTLY MY SOUL GREW STRONGER; HESITATING THEN NO LONGER,

Sir,

SAID I,

or Madam, truly your forgiveness I **implore;**

But the fact is I was napping, and so gently you came rapping,

And so faintly you came tapping, tapping at my chamber door,

That I scarce was sure I heard you.

HERE I OPENED WIDE THE DOOR;— DARKNESS THERE, AND NOTHING MORE.

DEEP INTO THAT DARKNESS PEERING, LONG I STOOD THERE WONDERING, FEARING, DOUBTING, DREAMING DREAMS NO MORTAL EVER DARED TO DREAM BEFORE;

BUT THE SILENCE WAS UNBROKEN, AND THE DARKNESS GAVE NO TOKEN,
AND THE ONLY WORD THERE SPOKEN WAS THE WHISPERED WORD,

Lenore!

THIS I WHISPERED, AND AN ECHO MURMURED BACK THE WORD,

Lenore!

MERELY THIS AND NOTHING MORE.

OPEN HERE I FLUNG THE SHUTTER,

WHEN, WITH MANY A FLIRT AND FLUTTER,
IN THERE STEPPED A STATELY RAVEN
OF THE SAINTLY DAYS OF YORE.

NOT THE LEAST OBEISANCE MADE HE;
NOT A MINUTE STOPPED OR STAYED HE;

BUT, WITH MIEN OF LORD OR LADY, PERCHED ABOVE MY CHAMBER DOOR—
PERCHED UPON A BUST OF PALLAS JUST ABOVE MY CHAMBER DOOR—
PERCHED, AND SAT, AND NOTHING MORE.

THEN THIS EBONY BIRD *BEGUILING* MY SAD FANCY INTO SMILING,
BY THE GRAVE AND STERN DECORUM OF THE *COUNTENANCE* IT WORE,

Though thy crest be shorn and shaven, thou,

I SAID,

art sure no craven,

Ghastly grim and ancient Raven wandering from the Nightly shore,—
Tell me what thy lordly name is on the Night's Plutonian shore!

QUOTH THE RAVEN,

Nevermore.

MUCH I MARVELED THIS UNGAINLY FOWL TO HEAR *DISCOURSE* SO PLAINLY,
THOUGH ITS ANSWER LITTLE MEANING—LITTLE RELEVANCY BORE;
FOR WE CANNOT HELP AGREEING THAT NO LIVING HUMAN BEING
EVER YET WAS BLESSED WITH SEEING BIRD ABOVE HIS CHAMBER DOOR—

BIRD OR BEAST UPON THE SCULPTURED
BUST ABOVE HIS CHAMBER DOOR,
WITH SUCH NAME AS "NEVERMORE."

BUT THE RAVEN STILL BEGUILING ALL MY SAD SOUL INTO SMILING,
STRAIGHT I WHEELED A CUSHIONED SEAT IN FRONT OF BIRD AND BUST AND DOOR;

THEN, UPON THE VELVET SINKING, I BETOOK MYSELF TO LINKING
FANCY UNTO FANCY, THINKING WHAT THIS OMINOUS BIRD OF YORE—
WHAT THIS GRIM, UNGAINLY, GHASTLY, GAUNT AND OMINOUS BIRD OF YORE
MEANT IN CROAKING

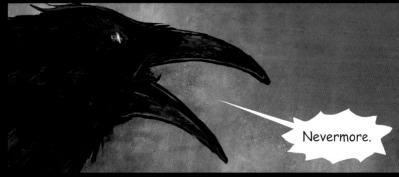

Nevermore.

THIS I SAT ENGAGED IN GUESSING,
BUT NO SYLLABLE EXPRESSING
TO THE FOWL WHOSE FIERY EYES NOW
BURNED INTO MY BOSOM'S CORE;
THIS AND MORE I SAT DIVINING, WITH
MY HEAD AT EASE RECLINING
ON THE CUSHION'S VELVET LINING
THAT THE LAMPLIGHT GLOATED O'ER,

BUT WHOSE VELVET
VIOLET LINING WITH
THE LAMPLIGHT
GLOATING O'ER
SHE SHALL PRESS,
AH, NEVERMORE!

THEN, METHOUGHT, THE AIR GREW DENSER, PERFUMED FROM AN UNSEEN CENSER SWUNG BY SERAPHIM WHOSE FOOT-FALLS TINKLED ON THE TUFTED FLOOR.

AND THE RAVEN, NEVER FLITTING,
  STILL IS SITTING, STILL IS SITTING
ON THE PALLID BUST OF PALLAS
  JUST ABOVE MY CHAMBER DOOR;
AND HIS EYES HAVE ALL THE
  SEEMING OF A DEMON'S THAT IS
  DREAMING,
AND THE LAMPLIGHT O'ER HIM
  STREAMING THROWS HIS SHADOW
  ON THE FLOOR;

AND MY SOUL FROM OUT
THAT SHADOW THAT LIES
FLOATING ON THE FLOOR
SHALL BE LIFTED—

nevermore!

Close Reading

Read. Talk. Write.

Why does the poet repeat the word "nevermore" so many times throughout the poem?

Use these response frames as you talk or write about the poem. Cite evidence from the text.

> The word "nevermore" means ...
>
> The author repeats the word so many times because ...

Re-read.

Answer these questions. Use text-based evidence.

> Who or what does the narrator think makes the tapping sounds on his door?
>
> On page 29, the narrator tells the raven to "take thy beak from out my heart, and take thy form from off my door!" What does he mean?